THE WITHERED BOY

ALSO BY
MARSHALL RYAN MARESCA

MARADAINE SAGA PHASE ONE

THE ZIAPARR CYCLE

THE DISPLACED DAUGHTERS

MARADAINE SAGA PHASE TWO

MARADAINE SAGA SHORTS

*- Forthcoming

PRAISE FOR
MARSHALL RYAN MARESCA

Maresca offers something beyond the usual high fantasy fare, with a wealth of unique and well-rounded characters, a vivid setting, and complicatedly intertwined social issues that feel especially timely.

— PUBLISHERS WEEKLY

I love the complexity of Marshall Ryan Maresca's worldbuilding as the vast conspiracy underlying all the inner workings of Maradaine is emerging through the intertwining pieces coming together. It's nothing short of brilliant!

— FRESH FICTION

It's a story about morality, about sacrifice, about what people want from life. It's a fun story—there's quips, swordfights, chases through the streets. It's a compelling, convincing work of fantasy, and a worthy addition to the rich tapestry that is the works of Maradaine.

— SCI-FI AND FANTASY REVIEWS

Marshall Ryan Maresca is one of the most ambitious fantasy authors to burst on the scene in the last decade.

— BLACK GATE MAGAZINE

Maresca continues his expert expansion of his intricately-crafted world, introducing fascinating new locations and vibrant characters while serving up a high-energy, magic-laced plot. *The Mystical Murders of Yin Mara* is a clever, captivating adventure.

— CASS MORRIS, AUTHOR OF
FROM UNSEEN FIRE

THE WITHERED BOY

MARSHALL RYAN MARESCA

A

ARTEMISIA

First Printing, November 2023

1 2 3 4 5 6 7 8 9

<u>Chronological Note</u>

The Withered Boy begins in the last decade of the twelfth century (by the Druth Calendar) and spans many years before ending in Oscan, 1215, approximately the same time as *People of the City*.

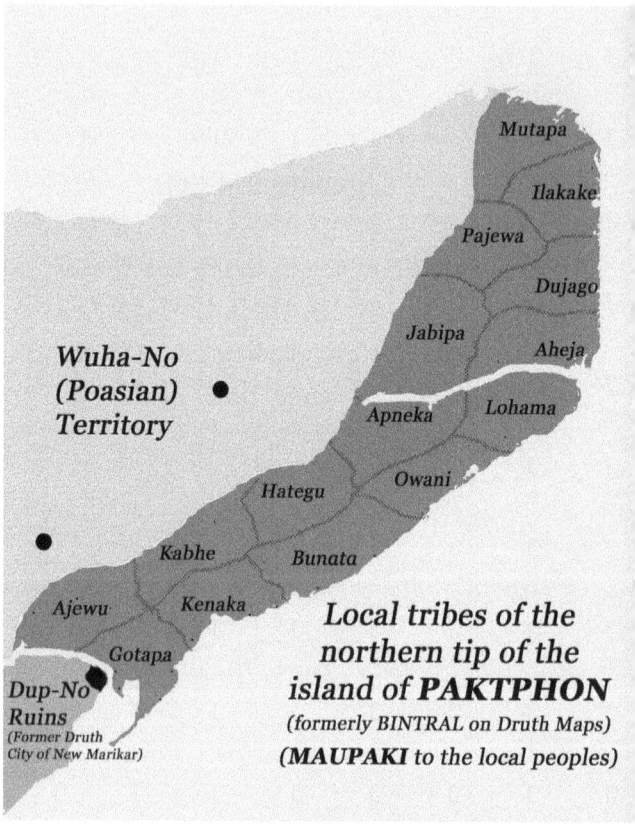

Mutapa

Ilakake

Pajewa

Dujago

Jabipa

Aheja

Wuha-No
(Poasian)
Territory

Apneka

Lohama

Owani

Hategu

Kabhe

Bunata

Ajewu

Kenaka

Gotapa

Dup-No
Ruins
*(Former Druth
City of New Marikar)*

**Local tribes of the
northern tip of the
island of PAKTPHON**
(formerly BINTRAL on Druth Maps)
(**MAUPAKI** to the local peoples)

CHAPTER I

Dabugo was abandoned on the beach the day he was born.

This was the custom of the Gotapa people whenever two babies were born from the same mother at once: one raised, one abandoned. Dabugo had been born with his left arm withered, curled and twisted, and he barely made any sound. His brother had strong hands and strong lungs filled with life. His brother would be the pride of the Gotapa people, and was named Habedo, "the bright light." Dabugo, "the withered one," was named, as was only proper, and then the villagers left him on the beach, where the tide or the birds would take him.

Neither the tide or the birds took him. No one had seen it, but it was believed that one of the village dogs had taken him up in her teeth like a pup and brought him back. He had been found the next day curled with a litter of pups, nursing from the mother dog.

The Gotapa took this as a sign that while they did not want him, the world needed him. He would serve some great purpose they did not understand. Therefore, they would do what they must to raise him, if nothing else. One day he would be old enough, strong enough, to walk away from the Gotapa. They would bring him to that day, and no further.

There were other peoples on the island, and it was considered that perhaps the purpose Dabugo would serve was for them. Up the shore, there were the Kenaka, with whom the Gotapa would trade; and the Bunata, with whom the Kenaka would fight. There were more peoples down the shore, and even more inland, living by the springs.

And then there were the paler peoples, not of the island, who were there to fight each other.

First, there were the ones whose skin was like the flesh of a potato, and among the Gotapa they were called the Dup-No, the potato people. What they called themselves sounded similar, and it was a good name for them. Many of them came to live on the island, building their own villages with stone walls. The Dup-No would come to the villages of the Gotapa, and they would often wear far too much cloth for the warm sun. They would sweat and their potato skin would turn the color of gaba berries. They would trade their cold tools, and lie with the Gotapa women, and children would be born who were neither dark like the Gotapa or pale like the Dup-No. Sometimes those children were left on the beach, and the Dup-No would scream and claim the babies, taking them back to their stone-wall villages.

The Dup-No were not of the island, but they had been there for many Seasons of Storm. Even the oldest among the Gotapa had known of the Dup-No their whole lives.

The other people had skin like the flesh of the coconut, and hair like the night. Wuha-No, the Gotapa called them. They did not call themselves that. They did not trade or lie with the Gotapa or any other local people. The Wuha-No were brutal, but not cruel. They would draw a line in the dirt and say that the land was theirs, and all who were not them must not cross the line. If one of the local people crossed the line, they were killed without hesitation or further warning.

The Dup-No said they were at war with the Wuha-No. They told the Gotapa and the other local people, this is our war, and you must not be part of it, or the Poasians— what they called the Wuha-No — would kill all the local peoples. They said it had happened before on other islands.

The pale peoples fought each other for many of Dabugo's youngest seasons.

Dabugo lived with different families, in different villages of the Gotapa, over the early seasons of his life. Most families saw this as a necessary burden. Dabugo was wanted by the world, but not the villages. They accepted he must be tended to, but there was little affection. Sometimes he would have to walk for miles to another village, where they knew him as "the burden of the Gotapa."

Most families rarely let him stay with them for more than one cycle of the red moon. Perhaps the white moon, if they were especially generous. They were rarely cruel about turning him out. They simply let him know he should find a different place to sleep. The worst was in the home of his own mother. She acknowledged he was of her flesh, that Habedo was his brother. But she was harsh, cold. He never stayed there more than a few days. Usually, his brother shoved him out into the open air in the middle of the night.

The one place he was allowed to stay longer, the closest he had to a home in the village, was with the woman Kapala. She was kinder than obligation required. She let him stay for several moon cycles at a time.

She had a regular companion, a soldier of the Dup-No, called Heck-Nell. Heck-Nell was a strange man, kind to Dabugo when he was around, and his kindness was not obligation.

He was kind to Dabugo because he was a kind man who liked children. He had a daughter with Kapala, and spent as much time as he was allowed in the village. Most of the other soldier-men of the Dup-no only visited for nights and returned to their fortress of stone, but Heck-Nell thought of Kapala and his daughter as family, and saw Dabugo as an extension of that family.

Unlike the men of the Gotapa, Heck-Nell enjoyed teaching Dabugo things.

He showed Dabugo about fishing, hunting, using a stone sling and a Dup-No knife. He wanted to show Dabugo about bows, but with only one good arm, Dabugo could never manage.

Heck-Nell never said it outright, as he spoke only a little of the Gotapa language, but Heck-Nell craved a son, and Dabugo was there for him.

Dabugo liked that, since no one else treated him like a wanted child. Dabugo knew it would not last. Nothing did.

"These people," Heck-Nell said once— his language rough and broken— while he chewed on the *evata* leaves that had ripened and turned violet. "They don't see you. They see responsibility. They see burden."

"I am a burden," Dabugo said.

"No, you're a boy." He said more in his native tongue, but Dabugo did not understand. Heck-Nell seemed very upset with the rest of the Gotapa. But Dabugo understood one thing from Heck-Nell— that however his people treated him, somewhere in the world was a place he was wanted.

When Dabugo had lived through seven passings of the Season of Storm, the war between the Dup-No and the Wuha-No ended, at least on his island. The Dup-No left their great villages with stone walls and ran for their ships. They took many of the children they had claimed off the beach.

Heck-Nell pleaded with Kapala to come with him. She refused, but did not stop him from taking the girl. Heck-Nell left the island with his daughter, to return to the homeland of the Dup-No.

None had tried to take Dabugo. He had whispered his hope for it into the wind, but the wind did not bring that hope back to him. That was not why the world wanted him. He stayed with the Gotapa, tended to, but unwanted.

The Dup-No were gone, and the Wuha-No remained. They drew many new lines in the dirt. The Gotapa villages were far from the lines the Wuha-No drew. They paid little mind to it.

Other villages did not have that luxury.

CHAPTER 2

S easons of storm came and passed. News would come that villages far away had fought each other, or that the Wuha-No had drawn new lines. Other villages would trade with the Gotapa, or try to start war with them. The Gotapa did not want war. They gave the Kenaka a potato field by the river so there would not be one. The other villages could fight each other, risk the anger of the Wuha-No, whatever they wished. The Gotapa would live their own lives.

Habedo had grown to the height of a man, one of the tallest in the village. Dabugo, despite being born on the same day, only had the stature of a boy. If he stood next to Habedo— a thing he would never do, since Habedo would push him into the sand whenever he came near—he would only come up to his chin.

And his one arm useless, a withered stump.

The other arm, Dabugo made as strong as stone. Every day, he would lift rocks and throw them. Every day, he taught himself the things he would need to survive. He knew the sling and the knife. He watched the other boys— especially Habedo— and saw how they would use their spears for fish or birds. He would go alone into the trees and practice all the things the other boys would do with each other.

He did these things in secret, because if anyone from the village saw that he was capable, they would decide that the day had come, and he would be sent away. He wasn't ready for that, not yet.

He taught himself to hunt birds, catch fish and forage for roots and fungi. He had to learn these things; he needed to feed himself beyond what the village would allow him. He was always hungry.

For some time, he had presumed he was always hungry because he was only fed the last scraps the village would spare him— the very least to keep him alive. But as he grew and ate more on his own, he realized that there was something different about him. Unless Habedo and the other boys were also sneaking off and eating more while hidden away, he was eating as much as they were, yet he was still constantly hungry.

Perhaps the other boys were as well. He did not speak to them about it. He spoke to very few people about anything. He asked Kapala once, but she told him he should keep it to himself, or the village would decide that this was the day and send him off.

Dabugo's fourteenth Season of Storm passed, and while the village had not sent him away, he was not welcome to sleep in any of the huts. Not even Kapala's.

"It cannot be, not anymore," she said. "You are not a child to be watched after. And you are not a man to be coupled with. It cannot be." When he pressed her, she just said, "Perhaps you should join your brother and the others born in your season."

Dabugo started watching these boys from a distance. They were not sleeping in the huts of their mothers either, not anymore. Instead, they slept on the beach, huddled together, and when the sun rose, they went off to the reefs all day.

Dabugo came to the beach in the nighttime, and waited for them to wake. As the sky turned gray with dawn, he crouched next to Habedo, sleeping on the edge of the group.

"Brother," he said quietly. "What are you all doing?"

Habedo opened his eyes, squinting at Dabugo. "We are the sleepers, alone and together. As is the way. Did no one tell you?"

Dabugo shook his head. "No one tells me things. You know this."

"Talk to your mewling keeper. Kapala."

"She said to speak to you."

Habedo sighed, sitting up. "She is a pest. As are you. This is not a thing for you. This is for those who will be the men of the Gotapa." He swung his arm at Dabugo's face, but Dabugo caught his hand and held it strong with his good arm.

"Right now, I am as you are, brother," Dabugo said.

"Do not call me that," Habedo said. "You do not have a place here. This is our place, until we are men."

"What do you all do on the reefs? Is that about becoming men?"

"Are you spying on us? Do you watch us like the Wuha-No?"

"I watch all things, brother."

Habedo got to his feet and shoved Dabugo. "I

am no brother to you. I am for the Gotapa, and you are for whatever your purpose is!"

The other boys were awake now, all on their feet. "Smash him, Habedo! Make him eat the sand!"

Habedo came at Dabugo, swinging his great, powerful arms in rage. And for a moment, Dabugo felt the same rage. But in that rage there came a stillness. For just a moment, the entire world stopped. Habedo was frozen in his charge. The other boys just as motionless and silent, their faces contorted with their jeers.

And in that moment, Dabugo could move, could strike back with as much rage as he could put into his arm.

And then the world came rushing back, and his blow knocked Habedo down into the ground.

The other boys gaped as Habedo found himself felled, face in the sand. Habedo popped up onto his feet, and first, he looked like he wanted to kill Dabugo. Then a smile crossed his face, a smile Dabugo did not trust.

"Perhaps we should show you," he said. "Let's bring him to the reef."

The boys laughed, clearly thinking Habedo was in jest. Habedo shushed them. "We were thoughtless, friends. He may not need to be a man of the Gotapa, but he must be a man. No?"

The other boys looked at each other in confusion. "As you say, Habedo."

"Yes," he said, turning back to Dabugo with hate in his eyes. "As I say."

The boys all went along the shore to a cove among the reefs. As they walked, Dabugo picked up a stone and secreted it in the small hand of his withered arm. He couldn't do much of anything with that hand, but it could hold onto a stone, so he'd have it at the ready if he needed to fight these boys. His heart told him a trick was coming, but despite that, he followed his curiosity.

"None of the fathers told you?" Habedo asked him as they came down to the water.

"None of the fathers speak to me," Dabugo said. "You know this. The most they do is talk about me while I stand there, as if I were a spirit of the wind that could not be seen."

"This is the way," Habedo said. "We are not children to be tended to any more. But we are not men of the village, ready to couple and father, as much as we want to."

"Do you feel that?" one of the other boys— Akeapu— asked Dabugo. "Do you swell as you see the girls and mothers work in the water or soil? Or are you withered down there like your arm?"

Dabugo knew what Akeapo meant— he had felt those very things— but he had never quite understood why those feelings had come upon him. "I am just like you in those things," he said, though he wondered how much he was lying.

"Then you understand," Habedo said, clapping Dabugo on the back. "Thus we must prove we are worthy."

"And how do we do that?" Dabugo asked.

"With that," Habedo said. The other boys ran ahead to a brush of trees, and pulled something out onto the beach. It was a boat— a small raft with a crude sail, not like the outriggers that the men of the village used. "We have built that with our own hands, and now we must bring back a fish."

"A fish?" Dabugo asked. "We have all caught many fish, since we were small."

"Even you?" Akeapu asked.

"I'm not talking about the fish of the streams or that swim in the shallows of the tides," Habedo said. He pointing out to the horizon. "I'm talking a great fish. One to feed the village."

"Those are from the deep ocean," Dabugo said.

"Exactly," Habedo said. "That's where we're going today, to show that we are men. Is that what you are?"

Fear filled his heart. Dabugo had never dared to even go on one of the boats past the breakers. He could never swim with much confidence.

"Of course, he isn't," Akeapo said. "He's at best half of one."

Even though a voice in his head told him to ignore Akeapo, to walk away, Dabugo's anger and heart took hold of him. "I am as much of one as any of you. As much as you spit on me, I am of this village, and will not be denied by you anymore." He tapped his finger on Akeapo's chest. Again, his anger rose and felt like it exploded from his hand. Akeapo cried out.

"Great ones above," Akeapo said. "No wonder his arm is withered away. All his strength is in the other arm."

"Then it is settled," Habedo said, and again that untrustworthy smile crept across his face. "You will join us on the water."

THE SAIL TOOK THE RAFT OUT IN THE WATER, PAST the breakers of the bay and to the open ocean. Dabugo's heart thundered in his chest, and he wasn't certain if it was terror or joy that gripped him. The salt in the air filled his nose as the wind whipped through his hair.

The other boys held onto ropes lashed to the mast with their left hands, while holding spears in their right. They took turns leaning over the edge to look down into the clear, blue water, laughing and jibing as they shot through the water.

"Your turn," Habedo told him.

Dabugo took the rope and tied it to his waist, and then took his place on the edge. He leaned out, so he could touch the water as it rushed by. He glanced down into the crystal water, seeing more fish swimming below than he had ever in his life. None of them were the great fish that he expected them to be hunting, but there were so many it seemed impossible to not spear one.

The boat lurched, and Dabugo's head went under. The rush of water slammed into his mouth and nose, and he never had a moment to take a breath. He struggled, unable to twist himself to reach the rope with his good arm, unable to pull himself out of the water.

Then the boat swerved again, and he flew up

out of the water and crashed back on the deck, surrounded by laughing boys.

"Did you see that?" Utaku cackled, lips and teeth stained purple. "His little twig arm flapping around!"

Dabugo could do little but cough up the water that had filled his lungs.

"You need to pull up when that happens!" Akeapo said. His lips had the same stain, and he laughed even harder than Utaku.

Dabugo looked up at all of them. Most of them had the purple stains on their lips, face, fingers.

"Are you—" he started, barely able to breathe through the salt and pain in his lungs. "Are you…"

"Did you spear one?" Utaku cackled. "Or did you lose your spear?"

"He didn't lose it!" another shouted.

Dabugo realized his spear was still in his hand, and he swung it against Utaku's leg, knocking the boy over. He struggled to get to his feet, despite still clawing through his lungs just for a breath, and the rocky sway of the boat. Utaku got back up as well, lunging at Dabugo. Habedo held the boy back, keeping him from striking Dabugo.

Habedo stood out from the others, in that his lips and teeth were not stained.

"They're all chewing *evata* leaves!" Dabugo shouted. That's why they had turned giddy, the leaves had them dreaming in the day. "You would risk that while on the water?"

"We are men!" Utaku said. "And we do what we wish!"

"You are all fools!" Dabugo said, throwing down his spear. "You are not out here to earn your manhood. You pretend you already have it!"

Akeapo's fist cracked into Dabugo's chin. "We are men, and you will never be. Not with us."

"Not with the Gotapa," Utaku said.

"Enough," Habedo said. "We are not here to fight him, we are here to prove what we are." He picked up his spear, and looked out to the horizon. "Time is short. The wind has shifted, and those clouds turn dark."

Dabugo rubbed his bruised face. "We should make back to land now."

"Swim back, cripple," Utaku said.

One of the other boys had already walked away from the rest of the group, hanging off the side with his spear at the ready. "I see one! I see one!" He dove into the water, letting go of his rope.

"Kanapi!" Habedo shouted. He pulled the sail

to turn the boat, but the rope snapped in his hands. The sail fell off its mast on top of the other boys.

"What did you do?" Utaku asked, pulling the sail off his head.

"I'm trying to get to Kanapi!"

"You cursed us! Bringing the cripple!"

Dabugo ignored them, going to the back of the boat, searching the water for Kanapi. But there was no sign of him. No sign of anything but water.

Dabugo could barely even see the island in the distance.

"Get it back up!" Habedo ordered. "We need to—"

Thunder cracked through the sky, and the dark clouds blocked the sun. Rain crashed down on them hard and fast.

Habedo grabbed one of the ropes and tied it around his waist, like Dabugo had, and dove into the water.

"What is he doing?" Utaku asked.

Dabugo saw— down in the deep, Kanapi was thrashing and lost. Habedo swam toward him, despite the boat pulling away as the storm winds smashed into it.

"We're going to die!" Akeapo cried. "We will drown and die!"

"It's his fault!" Utaku said, pointing at Dabugo. "Give him to the storm!"

He grabbed Dabugo's shoulders and hurled him into the water. Dabugo went under hard and fast, and he couldn't right himself with only one arm. Impossible with the wind and storm chopping the waves up.

But he was still lashed to the boat, and that rope kept him close. He reached out and grabbed the rope, pulling himself back up, out of the water and onto the boat.

He saw Habedo struggling to grab Kanapi's hand, and both of them were going to drown. Dabugo reached out and took hold of both of them, pulling them up on the boat as well.

The storm was all around them. They needed to get back to the island, before they all were killed. Out in the distance, he could see the island, so far away it was just a speck of green on the horizon.

He saw it, and reached out and grabbed it, pulling the whole boat toward the island.

It only then occurred to Dabugo that what he was doing was impossible. He was grabbing things far beyond the reach of his arm. Pulling, far beyond the strength of man.

Yet he was doing it. Holding the island and

pulling all of them toward it with something that was not his arm— either his good one or his withered one.

The boys all stared at him in horror as the boat whipped across the water, flying through the bay and smashing on the beach in front of their village. Dabugo and the others were hurled off the boat, landing in a pile of flesh on the sand.

Several of the elders of the village ran up, shouting and screaming. Kapala and the other mothers and fathers.

"What is this? What have you done?"

Dabugo could barely breathe, barely move. Whatever he had just done, it had taken all his strength. He felt he could eat an entire great fish, were it placed in front of him.

One of the elders grabbed Utaku by the face, pulling him to his feet. "Trying to get the big fish, hmm? Trying to be men, before your time? And chewing the *evata* like giddy fools!"

"Stupid boys!" another said.

"But what is this?" Kapala asked, pointing to the boat, wedged into the sandbank. She looked at the boys. "No sail could drive a boat with such speed, like a striking bird."

Habedo stood up, looking at the elders and then back at Dabugo. "We— we were on the

water, and we were going to drown. And then—
then he——- he became filled with light, and that
light pulled us to safety."

"The withered one," one elder said. "He has
found his purpose. Today is the day."

CHAPTER 3

The firepit in the center of the village was a place of sanctity. It was where people gathered for stories, news, or celebration. When a father or mother died, or a new baby was born, or a child became a man, the made the announcement was made at the firepit. Whether or not a fire burned there, it was the place where the breathing heart of the Gotapa was found.

Today, the fire was out, though embers of char still glowed as the sky turned dark from the coming storm. Dabugo stood at the edge of the pit, the wisps of warmth doing very little to ease the chill in his bones, the emptiness in his stomach. Kapala had, at least, brought him dried fish and potatoes. Others objected to this, but she stared at them with hard, baleful eyes until they silenced.

"We have waited and endured," Magode, Father of Fathers said. "Many seasons ago, a boy was placed on the beach to be taken by the waves, but the world saved him, so he must have a purpose."

"I know the story," Dabugo said.

"Quiet," another elder said to him.

"We did not know this purpose, but we knew it was our duty to tend to him until he was ready to face it. Until he was strong enough to be in the world alone."

"Today is the day," one of the mothers said.

"Today is the day," another said.

"Why is today the day?" Kapala asked. Dabugo knew she was screaming into the wind— the decision had been made— but he appreciated that she stood for him. "Because he is touched with a gift?"

"He pulled a boat across the water! He is not a natural boy!"

"He has an unseen hand," Magode said. "Perhaps that is why his natural one is useless. But this unseen hand has great strength. He has great strength, and the world needs it. It is his purpose."

"Where?" Dabugo asked. "Where do you expect me to go?"

"Away from here," Magode said. "You are not

of the Gotapa. You are of the world. So now walk away, and find your place."

"A storm is about to crash!" Kapala shouted. "You would send him out in that? You would have such smoke in your lungs? Such stone in your hearts?"

"Today is the day," Magode said. "We all agreed, we would bring him to this point, and no further."

Dabugo touched Kapala on the shoulder. "They are stone and smoke. And it matters not." Fear and anger burned in his stomach, but he would not argue or cause Kapala trouble. "I have been endured by the Gotapa, and I have endured all of you. Almost to the body, you have been little more than tolerant of your duty to me, and now it is done. May the stone in your hearts not weigh too heavy when you finally rest."

"You do not—" Magode said, striding up to Dabugo like he was going to strike him.

"I say what I will," Dabugo said. "Today is my day. I am now a man, and I will go. I will take a spear and a bundle of cloth, a skin of water and food for my journey. The last duty you will perform for me."

"You would speak to us thus?" another elder asked. Not just any elder— the mother of

Dabugo's birth. It was the first thing she had said to him in seasons beyond his counting. It mattered not. He may have slept beneath her heart once, but now she was no one to him.

"I speak as you deserve," Dabugo said. "Bring what I need to me, and I will be gone."

The elders and other onlookers departed. Kapala remained for a moment, cradling his face. "I'm cursed to lose them all," she said. "My little girl, and now you."

"Your heart is filled with air and fire," Dabugo said. "It does you credit, and it will lift you when you take your final sleep."

Habedo approached, carrying a spear and a bundle of things. "I've brought you what you asked for," he said.

"Thank you," Dabugo said, taking them. "I'm sorry today was not what you wanted."

"Nor what you wanted," Habedo said. He took a moment, and then said, "You pulled me out of the water, and for that I am grateful. I will not forget."

"Maybe that has been my purpose," Dabugo said. "To save you, so the Gotapa would have you now."

Habedo shook his head. "We shared a mother, sat under her heart together, yet there is nothing alike between us. Now you must go. Made a man before I was."

"You're wrong," Dabugo said. "I have not become a man. Not in their eyes. I am merely strong enough to be forced to go. I will never be a man to them."

"Then to me," Habedo said. "If that has value."

It was the kindest thing Habedo had ever said to him. "It does."

There was no more to say, and the storm was coming. Dabugo would have to move quickly to make it to the shelter he had already built, hidden away from the village.

This day had been coming. Even though he wasn't ready, he was prepared.

———◆———

Dabugo wandered for several days, laying low in the outskirts of the Gotapa lands. His village would not take him, nor would the other villages of the Gotapa. Sooner or later, he would be found, and they might do terrible things to him.

He thought about traveling away from the sun, to the lands of the Ajewu or Kanaka or beyond, but he feared they would mark him as a Gotapa and, at best, shun him. Perhaps even hurt him.

He could not fight them. He was not as strong as the village believed. He may have an unseen hand— now that he understood that, he could feel it, he could sense that it was a part of him— but he didn't know how to use it. He didn't understand how he had done those things on the boat.

He could not rely on it.

He considered walking toward the sunset, away from all the villages. That was where the Wuha-No lived. He wondered if the stories really were true: that the Wuha-No were as fearsome as he had been told. They might not care that one withered villager from the Gotapa wandered into their lands and made a simple life for himself.

But it was true the Wuha-No would kill, without pity. He did not dare risk it.

So he went toward the midday sun, to the places the Dup-no abandoned. The Gotapa and other tribes did not dare go there, and the Wuha-No left it alone. All of them saw that place as tainted, damaged by the Dup-No and their strange cities of stone.

An unwanted place. Exactly where Dabugo belonged.

He went toward the midday sun until he reached the river— a terrible rushing river with swirls of white and hidden rocks. Many strong boys who thought they swam well had their heads dashed in that water. Dabugo knew he could not swim well.

He wandered up the riverbank until he came upon a Dup-No structure. It was not stone, but wood and lashed rope— a simple bridge across the river. Many Seasons of Storm had passed since the Dup-No had left, and the ropes were dry and brittle, the wood weak and worn.

Still, it was the only way he saw to cross.

He took a cautious step on to the first plank of wood. It creaked and groaned under his weight, and he didn't feel he could fully trust it. But he didn't see any other way. He took another step, and a third, but his confidence in the security of the bridge did not increase.

A few more steps, and one of the ropes snapped. The entire bridge shuddered, but still held. Out of fear, Dabugo reached out with his unseen hand to grab a tree on the opposite side of the river, pulling it out of the ground.

He let it go, taking a moment to breathe. He couldn't let himself be careless or reckless with his unseen hand, whatever it was or whatever it meant.

But it was strength, and he'd be a fool to ignore it. It was his purpose, he was certain of that.

Breathing slowly, he closed his eyes and reached out with the unseen hand. He could feel it more easily now, a part of him that had been asleep.

Another rope of the bridge snapped.

He refused to let himself lash out on instinct again. Instead, he opened his eyes and picked himself up with his unseen hand. It made no sense that he could do so, but he hovered a few inches above the rotten wood slats.

He then pushed himself forward, until he was over solid ground, and let himself drop down to his feet.

He collapsed to his knees. Doing that took more strength than he realized. He tore into his bag and ate the dried meat and fruit he had in there. All of it, before he realized what he was doing. Even that didn't satisfy him, but it let him get back to his feet.

Dabugo walked back down the riverbank, heading toward the shore, where the stone walls of the abandoned Dup-No city stood. The walls were crumbling, and the tiled walkways cracked, plants growing through the stone— but much of the place seemed to be intact. There were several buildings with solid walls and roofs. These stone places of the Dup-No were odd, but held up to the seasons of storm.

Dabugo found one place, which still had a few Dup-No things inside. Blankets, clothes, and tools. A firepit inside the room. Dabugo was cold and weary, so he decided this was a good place to rest until he knew what he would do next. He gathered some dry wood and lit a fire in the firepit— with his own hand, not the unseen one. But he imagined that he could create a fire with his unseen hand. Somehow, he understood that was a thing he could do, if he just pushed the right way.

He wrapped a few potatoes in green leaves and buried them in the ashes of the firepit. In the morning, they would be soft, crispy and delicious. He lay down on the Dup-No blanket and closed his eyes.

A sound intruded on his sleep, and he opened his eyes to see another pair staring back at him. Eyes of sickly blue, like the sky after a storm had passed. Eyes belonging to a woman, whose skin was pale and drawn, like the flesh of the coconut.

A Wuha-No. A Poasian.

CHAPTER 4

For a moment, Dabugo thought this woman was an actual corpse, alert and walking, like in the stories some fathers would tell to frighten children. Her appearance filled him with fear. She was as pale as death, and so thin and drawn one could see the shape of the bones in her face and shoulders.

Then she spoke, harsh and rapid. The words were like the river as it crashed through the rocks; they sounded like they hurt her mouth as much as they did his ears.

"Stop," he pleaded. "I just want to rest alone."

She spoke more, and pointed to the fire. Then she pointed out the door.

"The fire?" he asked, pointing to it.

She repeated his word, then said another word,

bringing her hand up. She then pointed to the door, and then her eyes. "Poasia *kheig.*"

Dabugo thought he understood. "The smoke. They'll see the smoke. But aren't you—" He pointed to her.

She snarled at him, and then waved her hand again. But this time, when she did, the fire went out completely. Snuffed as if the rains had crashed on it. And when she did, Dabugo felt a sharp pull in his stomach.

She had an unseen hand as well.

"*Mnya,*" she said quietly, putting her hand over his mouth. He was about to protest, but she put her other hand over her own, pointing at the door.

Very softly, Dabugo heard steps outside.

She made another motion, and Dabugo felt another pull at his gut— at his unseen hand. The air shimmered around them, like a morning fog. Before Dabugo could say anything else, someone else came into the building. The woman clutched Dabugo even tighter to her, and while he wanted to shove away from her, this new stranger made him even more afraid. This one, garbed in black cloth, except his chest, draped in the same shining stone of the Dup-No tools. He also carried a large blade, black and shining.

The Wuha-No warrior glanced about the room, but gave no sign that he saw either of them. He frowned and left.

The woman held Dabugo in that tight embrace, hand over his mouth, for several minutes, and despite himself, despite his fear, Dabugo felt himself swell. This was the first time any woman had touched him in a way other than the way a mother would a child, and he had no idea how to react to that.

Then she released him, and in that same moment he released himself. She did not seem to notice or care, as she waved her hand and made the fog vanish. She stepped away, letting out a heavy breath, and then dropped to her knees.

Dabugo struggled to catch his own breath, calm his thundering heart. "They chased you?" he asked.

She looked at him in confusion, and then tried to say something, but she seemed to be too tired to even speak.

Dabugo was also tired, but more importantly, he was hungry. He didn't know how long he had slept, but it was now light outside. Morning had come, bringing this strange woman.

He went to the firepit, and dug in the ashes for the potatoes. Thankfully they hadn't been stolen, and were still warm. He unwrapped one and hungrily bit into it. Crisp and soft and delicious.

The woman stared at him, her eyes filled with hunger. He handed her one of the potatoes. She tore into it, eating the ashy leaves and the potato all at once. He gave her another, eating his second as well. He shouldn't be giving his food to her so readily, but he knew where to find more potatoes. They were simple to find, and probably quite plentiful in the abandoned stone city.

He took his water skin out of his pack and drank a few sips, and gave it to her. She took that eagerly as well. After drinking and eating, she sat up and looked at him with a strange regard, as if only now was she really taking note of him.

"Cfradja," she said, pointing to herself before pointing to him.

Presuming she was giving him her name, he did the same. "Dabugo," he said, tapping his chest.

"Dabugo," she confirmed, touching him again.

"Cfradja," he said back to her, touching her gently. It wasn't easy for him to say, but she made a shake of her head that looked like agreement or amusement.

"So they chased you?" he asked again. "You don't want to go back with them?"

She frowned and said something harsh and rolling.

He tried simpler. "Poasians... not your friends?"

"Poasia," she said angrily, and then spat on the ground. That was clear enough.

Dabugo smiled. "So you're an exile as well."

———————

DAYS FOLLOWED, AND THE POASIANS DID NOT return. Dabugo kept an easy distance from Cfradja, letting her find her own way in the ruins of the Dup-No city.

After Dabugo was convinced that no other Poasians were coming, for him or her, and that there was no further immediate danger he went to work making this place his home. He gathered fruit and potatoes, speared fish in the river, caught the squawking flightless birds that wandered around the city, and made the house he had selected into a place of comfort and rest.

He watched Cfradja try to do the same, but she did not seem to know where to find fruit or potatoes, and could not spear fish, and chased the flightless birds with little success. Once in a while, she would lash out with her unseen hand, catching the bird or the fish that way, but she seemed even more angered and upset by doing that.

Dabugo made a basket out of frond leaves, and filled it with fruit, potatoes, salted fish and eggs, and left it outside the house Cfradja claimed. Later that day, he saw that she had taken it.

The next morning, when he went out to the river with his spear, she was waiting for him. She had her own spear— shine-stone tipped— and gestured to him, then it, and then the river. She spoke, and he didn't understand what she said, but he took her meaning, after a fashion. She wanted him to teach her to catch the fish.

He pointed to her, and then summoned forth the glow of his unseen hand. He hoped she understood what he was asking of her. "You teach me that, as well. We teach each other."

She gave him a slight smile, and showed him her open hand. That seemed to mean a yes.

The days went like this— they would hunt and gather together, and during that time they would both speak, slowly gaining each other's tongues. She tried to show him how to make use of his invisible hand, but that was harder to achieve at first. But slowly, over time, Dabugo gained understanding of how he could use it and control it.

Over time, they stayed in the same house, did everything together. They would hunt, and gather, and build the things they needed. They would prepare the food, they would practice using the unseen hand. They would talk to each other and slowly learn each other's tongues. They would lie together to sleep, and couple like the mothers and fathers of the village. Everything.

Except for eating. Other than that first time when he gave her the potatoes, she never ate in his presence. He learned that it was something she considered vile, taboo, and he showed his respect to her by not eating in front of her either.

"Dabugo," she said one morning as they laid a net in the river to catch fish. She had learned enough of his tongue to tell him basic things, but she spoke in her own, which he understood better than she did his. "Why were you cast out of your village? Was it your arm?"

"It was not," he said, using her tongue. It was hard to speak, but he found it a worthy challenge. "Not directly. I was born with a brother, both sleeping under the same heartbeats of our mother."

"Twins," she said.

"A feared thing among my people. The tradition is the weaker child is left on the beach for the water to take. So I was left."

"And I thought the Poasians were cruel," she said.

This had always confused him, but he hadn't had enough command of her language to express his concerns before. "You say that like you are not one of them."

"No, I—" she had a flash of anger. "I'm not Poasian, I'm Cthellian."

"Cthell is a different tribe?" he asked.

"Something like that. Poasians control us, rule over us."

"Much like here."

"Much like here," she said. "When they determined I had a talent for magic—" that was her word for the unseen hand— "I was put into training and programs. For them. They decided I was needed for a project here."

"A purpose," Dabugo said.

"You could say that," she said. "A purpose of magical… corruption. Alteration. Torture." Dabugo didn't fully understand these words—these were things that didn't exist in his language. "They wanted to change me, and when I realized how, I knew I would rather die here in the wild than live through that."

"We both had purposes thrust upon us by others," he said quietly. She looked at him with curiosity, as if her very eyes were compelling him to continue. "When I survived being left on the beach, the village believed I was to serve a purpose. They kept me alive until I was strong enough to live on my own, so I would fulfill that purpose."

"I know your purpose," she said with a smile, touching his face. "You helped keep me alive. You help keep me safe from the Poasians. And you are strong with magic—"

"You are much better."

"I have training— you have raw power. Like I've never seen. So when they come back—"

"They have not come back."

"When they come back, we will be ready."

"Then our purpose was to find each other," he said as he caressed her arm. "A purpose I have such gratitude for."

CHAPTER 5

As the seasons passed, so did more of the village fathers, and more eyes looked to Habedo for guidance and leadership. At first, he relished this— he was eager to show them he was a worthy man, a worthy father for the village, and that he had a purpose among them that it was his duty to fulfill.

As the seasons passed, the Wuha-No drew new lines, and the lands the Ajewu and Kabhe lived on to now belonged to the Wuha-No. The Ajewu pushed closer to the beach, as did the Kabhe, to lands where the Kenaka and Gotapa lived.

As the seasons passed, the Gotapa clashed with the Ajewu and the Kenaka, and more fathers were lost, especially in villages away from the sun. Those villages cried for anyone who could hunt and fight to come help them, and Habedo answered the call.

After several seasons, Habedo had earned respect and glory fighting for his new village. He was now one of the village fathers, and his voice was heard above all others in matters of defending themselves from the Ajewu and Kabhe. It was a hard life, but one that he cherished, and he relished the position he held among his people.

Over those several seasons, he rarely thought of his brother, but when he did, he wondered what sort of purpose he was filling, and what having a grand destiny must be like. Did he take a boat off this island, to the lands where the Dup-No or Wuha-No came from? Did he walk and live in the larger world, a life far more important that a father and keeper of a Gotapa village? Did Dabugo think this life of Habedo's was frightfully simple and meaningless?

Habedo chased those thoughts away, but even then he would see his brother in his dreams. Every night he drowned, every night Dabugo pulled him out of the ocean. Every night, Dabugo would whisper in his ear, words he could never remember.

"Habedo, wake." Those words came through the dream, bringing him back to the solid world.

Iake, the mother he had taken to sharing his nights with, was over him, her hand on his chest.

"Was I disturbing you?" he asked. She had long been forgiving of his troubled sleep.

"No, others are outside the hut," she said. There was urgency in her voice.

"Is the sun even up?"

"Barely," she said.

He rose and followed her out. The morning was a dark haze, a cool fog had settled on the village. Several of Habedo's trusted friends were outside, all harried and hurt. Enopo was bleeding from his head, and Awijo was being carried by two others, blood pouring out of the gash in his belly.

"What has happened?"

Awijo spoke, despite struggling to breathe. "They came and attacked us in the harvest field. More than we could count."

"Who?" Habedo asked. Iake must have sensed what Habedo would need, as she emerged from the hut with his spear and sling.

"The Ajewu," one of them said.

"No, the Kabhe."

"Fools," Awijo said between his struggled breaths. "It was both together. They've claimed our harvest field, and they will come here."

"Then we must—" Habedo said, but he did not finish his thought. In the distance, through the fog and the brush of the forest, he saw the light of torches. First, just a few, and then more, in numbers that boggled his mind.

———

"WE NEED TO RUN," HABEDO SHOUTED. He turned to Iake, "Help get people out of the village, especially the elders and the children."

"Where?" she asked.

"To the river village," he said. Turning to the others, he said. "Those who must, run with them. Those who can, stand with me to hold the invaders back."

Several of the men around him tapped their spears on the ground. They were ready.

The forest was alight with fire now. They were coming hard and strong, and in moments the village would be overrun.

"I must tell you all this," Habedo said to his fellows. "This is not a fight we win. This is a fight we survive, if we are favored. Nothing more. Run when you must. Protect the others. Help them to the river."

"And what do we do when we reach the river?"

Habedo had no chance to answer, as a wave of the Kabhe came bursting though the treeline, armed with torches and heavy blankets. Habedo whipped a stone at their leadfather, who held up his blanketed arm to protect himself. The stone bounced off the blanket harmlessly.

That did not matter to Habedo, who had already leaped onto the leadfather with his spear raised. He did not try to stab with a straight thrust — the blanket would slow him down too much. Instead he spun his weapon and cracked it against the torch. The leadfather lost grip of the torch just long enough for Habedo to press him, knock the torch into the blanket. Suddenly, the leadfather was ablaze, and Habedo kicked him into his other men, spreading the fire to more of them.

But more of the Kabhe came from the trees, as did the Ajewu. They fought with desperate savagery, and it was clear why. Many were deathly thin, no muscle beneath their skin. They had to take the harvest fields of the Gotapa, or they would die.

Some set fire to the great hut near the center of the village. Habedo ran to them, slaying the fire starters with his spear, and he charged into the great hut.

"What is this horror?" Old Amipawa cried out as she lay on the ground in the great hut. Many of the elders spent their nights here, and Amipawa must have been left behind when the others ran. Habedo scooped her up over his shoulder.

"We must flee," he said. "I'm sorry I cannot do more."

He ran with her, following the trail that Iake and the others had left. Some of his fellow warriors were with him, but many had fallen in the battle.

"Habedo!" he heard Iake call from some ways away. "We are here!"

He found them in a clearing on the riverbank — Iake and several of the children, as well as a handful of young mothers and fathers, all looking scraped and hurt. Few of the elders had made it, save for Amipawa.

"They are still coming," one of his warriors said, pointing through the brush back to the village. Plumes of smoke filled the sky, and the war chants of the Kadhebo echoed through the air.

"They have the village, they have the fields, what more do they want?"

"Our deaths," Amipawa said. "There is only

so much to hunt, so much to harvest, and they need the Gotapa to die so they may live."

"We cannot fight, we must hide."

All eyes were on Habedo. He must be the last of the keepers, the father who must lead. So be it.

"On the other side of the river—"

"The despoiled places of the Dup-No?" Amipawa asked. "The land is cursed."

"And we will not be followed there," he said. He knew of a place where the river was shallow and gentle, and pointed them all that way.

But still the Ajewu and Kabhe screamed for blood and death, and still they came closer.

When they reached the shallow place of the raging river, the sun was high, the fog burned off, but the air was still a haze of smoke.

"Take them across," he told Iake. "I will cover our retreat until we are safe."

Iake led the children and the elders across the river— slowly and cautiously. The survivors of the village were halfway across when the Ajewu came.

"If there are no lands for the Ajewu, then there will be no Gotapa!" the Ajewu keeper shouted, raising his spear. "All of them shall fall!"

The Ajewu pounded their spears on the ground, a thunder of death about to fall.

"Go," Habedo told his other warriors, raising his spear. "Get them safe."

He would stand on this riverbank and save as many of his people as he could.

That would be his purpose. He whispered a quiet hope into the wind that he would be enough, that his people would live.

The Ajewu keeper screamed, and they all threw their spears.

Too many spears.

But the spears suddenly stopped mid-flight, as if the very air had turned to stone. They fell to the ground in a clatter, not one of them reaching the Gotapa. Had the wind answered his hopes?

Then a voice thundered through the air. It seemed to come from the very soul of the land, filling Habedo up through his bones.

"Begone!" the voice shouted. "Leave these people be!"

Habedo was frozen with fear, but whatever terror he felt was nothing compared to what gripped the Ajewu. They screamed and ran into the woods.

"Come." The same voice, but now quieter, right next to Habedo. He turned to see a man and woman— the woman as pale and thin as the dead.

A Wuha-No. And the man with one arm withered to a stump.

"Dabugo?" Habedo asked.

"Come," his brother said. "Let's get your people safe."

———◆———

Safe on the other side of the riverbank, on the supposedly ruined land of the Dup-No, Habedo rested with his people. He had several injuries from the battle— he hadn't even noticed them in the heat of the fight— and one of the mothers was tending to his wounds. Others rested in the stone huts of the Dup-No ruins, and food and water were passed around.

Food and water that came from Dabugo and his pale woman. Why were they here, and why did they have so much food?

"They say you are the high father and keeper of their village," Dabugo said as he came over with a basket of fruit. He was surprisingly adept with just one arm— carrying a spear, the basket and a war blanket all at once. He placed the basket next to Habedo. "You are to be commended. It's what you wanted."

"What I wanted?" Habedo asked. "I am the high father of a lost people with no village. And the rest of the Gotapa will face the same."

"I suppose they will," Dabugo said with a detached air.

"You don't care?"

"I didn't say that," Dabugo said.

"They are your people!"

"They are?" Dabugo sat down and shook his head. "I recall them making it quite clear I was not one of them."

"You were raised—"

"Begrudgingly."

That was an odd word to Habedo, and he didn't understand what Dabugo meant. "You were born there, in that village, under the same heart as me. However you were treated, that is your blood."

"And I was pushed away."

"Because you had a purpose!" Habedo shouted, getting to his feet, almost knocking over the mother tending to him. "And what has that been? Where have you been?"

Dabugo didn't answer.

"You've just been here, haven't you? Skulking around these ruins with that strange woman?"

"Cfradja."

"What?"

Dabugo got to his feet. "Her name is Cfradja. She's an exile, like me."

"She's a Wahu-No?"

"She's a victim of them. We've lived together, taught each other."

"Taught what?" Habedo pushed closer to his brother. "Does she have an unseen hand as well?"

"It's called magic."

"Sounds like a Wahu-No word. Is that more of what you've been doing? Learning to talk and act like a Wahu-No?"

"They're called— it doesn't matter." He walked away.

"It does matter," Habedo said, chasing after him. "Who you are— who you were supposed to be. I can't believe it was this."

"Do you even care?" Dabugo spat back at him. "When have you wasted a thought to what might have happened to me when I was chased out?"

"All the time," Habedo said, surprised at readily he confessed it, and by the hot tears that came to his eyes. "I imagined you finding your great purpose, when I had to be content with my simplicity."

"My great purpose?" Dabugo asked. "A joke,

and excuse. A reason to throw me to the elements."

"And you thrived!" Habedo spotted the pale woman, cautiously approaching. "And you met her. She has this 'magic'? And she taught you?"

"Yes," Dabugo said. The pale woman came up to him, wrapping her arm around his waist. A clear sign: she was the mother to his father then. It was odd to Habedo— in his belly, it felt wrong. But he swallowed that down. "Then think on this, brother: why did you find each other, were it not for your great purpose? You had a gift, one which you can use."

Dabugo's brow creased. "Tell me, what do you think my great purpose is? So I would be here to save you, your village?"

"Perhaps. Perhaps all the Gotapa."

"I cannot believe that."

"Wait," the woman said. "Why did the other tribes attack you?"

"They're starving. They were pushed out of their lands by your people," Habedo said.

"They are not mine," she said. "But that is their way. Take what they want, and convince their victims to make enemies of each other."

"But the Poasians are the enemy," Dabugo

said. He looked at Habedo, a light in his eye now. "I think I understand, brother."

"What do you understand?"

"My purpose," Dabugo said. "My purpose for all the people on this island."

CHAPTER 6

"GATHER SOME FIGHTERS," DABUGO TOLD HIS brother. "Only four or five, but the most intimidating ones you have. The rest of these people, send to our old village on the beach."

"Do you have a plan of some sort?" Habedo asked.

"I do," Dabugo said. He went to the riverbank and scooped up a handful of mud. "Cfradja, help me please?"

"What do you need?" she asked.

"Paint my face with the mud, and then shift its color to look unnatural. Then do the same to yourself."

"Of course," she said, and got to work with the mud.

"What are you doing?" Habedo asked.

"She and I will make ourselves look like nothing seen before. We cannot be Gotapa for what we will do, or seem to be part of you. We must be other. Thus we paint ourselves." Dabugo said.

"I meant, what will you do once you've dressed for battle?"

Dabugo let a smile cross his face— Habedo understood the purpose. "We need to go to the Ajewu, the Kadhebo, The Kanaka, and any other peoples as you travel up the coast. All of them, if we must."

"To what end?"

"To join together against the Poasians."

"The— who?"

"The Wahu-No," Dabugo said. He had forgotten that there were so many words, so many names for things, that he had learned in his life with Cfradja, that his brother and the rest of the Gotapa would never know. "They will eventually take the entire island for themselves, unless we stop them now. And that is my purpose."

"How is that?"

Dabugo chuckled as Cfradja finished with the mud on his face. "It's a thing I can do only because I am not of the Gotapa, brother. They said I was for the world, but I see now, I am for our island. All the people of the island. They need someone who is not of any tribe, who can be for all of them. Who else but me?"

Cfradja gathered her energy, touching his face with wisps of magic. He could feel the mud shift and change, and Habedo took a step back, staring in wonderment and horror.

"How does it look?" Dabugo asked.

"Like the sky and ocean are upon your face," he said.

"And like no people of any tribe," Dabugo said. "For my plan to work, I must be of no people, and thus of all people."

Cfradja did the same to her own face, giving it streaks of bright blue mud, sparkling with shining crystals. "So we are to go together?"

"We do not leave each other," he said. "As always." He looked to Habedo. "Gather your people."

Habedo went off. Cfradja watched Dabugo for a while, her blue eyes piercing him.

"You're certain you want to do this? We've been safe for years."

"Should we be merely safe, while others suffer?" he asked her. "Is that a valuable life?"

"It is a life," she said. "He's rattled you."

"Because he's right," Dabugo said. "I was

spared as an infant so I could serve a purpose. It's time I did that." He rinsed the mud off his hand. "I presumed you would join me, and that was improper to think without asking. You do not need to if you don't wish to."

"Where else would I go?" she said. "Back to the Poasians? With the elders and children of the tribes? Stay here alone? All of those are horrid. By your side, happily."

"And I'm happy to be by yours," he said. He said the words, and while he felt fond affection for Cfradja, he wondered how much of what they shared was merely due to circumstance. They were alone together in a world that hated them. She was happy to be at his side because there was nowhere else in the world for her. Or for him.

He had only saved Habedo and his people because he could. To show Habedo that he was stronger now. And perhaps that was why he was about to move forward with this mad scheme.

He didn't care about bringing the tribes together. He certainly didn't care if the Poasians killed everyone else on this island.

But he cared about showing Habedo he was better.

Habedo returned with a handful of his fighters.

"Come," Dabugo told Cfradja as they approached. "Let's go end this madness."

———◄———

DABUGO TOOK THE LEAD AS THEY WALKED TO Ajewu territory, with Cfradja at his left. She had always, on instinct, taken the position to defend his weak side. He always appreciated having her there. If nothing else, his exile had brought him to her, and his life had been richer and grander with her being in it.

And not just for the language, or the magic lessons, or even the coupling like they were a mother and father together— though no child ever came from it. Her very presence brought him peace. He hoped that she felt the same.

It was not a thing they spoke of.

They approached Habedo's fallen village, which was a smoking ruins. The Ajewu seemed to prefer to destroy the village completely than use what the Gotapa had built. Why was it people were afraid to use the ruins of failed or defeated peoples? Dabugo never understood that.

"Strike now!" someone shouted from the

canopy of trees. Several men came running out, throwing spears.

Dabugo reached out with his magic, and Cfradja did the same— their magic flowed in perfect concert, like she was his left arm and knew exactly what he needed. The spears burst into flame and turned into ash in the air.

Dabugo put his magic into his voice. "We are not here to fight you. We could render you to the salt of the sea if we wished, but we seek to talk."

One of the Ajewu came forward. "Talk of what, strange ones?"

Dabugo stepped forward, Cfradja right by his side. "We are not of the Gotapa, but we are here with their people. We would have some of yours — those who are empowered to talk— to come with us."

"To talk of what?"

"To talk with the Kabhe, and the Kenaka, the Bunaka, the Hategu, the Apneka and Owani and Jabipa— and all the peoples who are from this island."

"She is not of this island."

"No," Dabugo said. "She is of a people who are just as much a victim of the Wuha-No as we all are on this island."

"We do not need to talk," the Ajewu said. "We fight, and we take new lands for ourselves."

"Idiocy," Dabugo said. "You take land from the Gotapa, Kenaka or Kabhe, who should be your allies."

"We take what we need."

"Like the Poasians," Cfradja said with scorn, in her own tongue.

"What did that pale beast say?"

"She said you were like the Wuha-No," Dabugo said. "And we should be like them— we should be like them and draw a line that they shall not cross. We should make them fear the peoples of this island, and know that they stay here by our good graces."

"And how do you propose to do that? With an army led by him?" The Ajewu pointed to Habedo.

"He will fight for this island, as will I," Dabugo said. "Will you? Will your people?"

The Ajewu keeper scoffed, but one of the others asked. "How can we stand against the Wuha-No?"

"Together," Dabugo said. "I am not one of any of you. But I will stand with all of you."

"You?" the Ajewu keeper shouted. "A withered half-man and his pale skeleton of a mother?"

Cfradja lashed out, a storm of cloud and lightning launching out in a claw that grabbed the Ajewu leader and lifted him off the ground. "I will fight the Poasians at his side. I will fight for the people of this island," she snarled. "I was not born here, and I was brought here against my will, but I will do right by it and its people."

Habedo stepped forward. "Come, Ioaheaka," he said. Clearly, he knew the Ajewu keeper. "Are we to be shamed by this foreign woman, who is willing to do more than all of us to protect our elders, mothers and children? Or do we join the Withered Man and the Pale Woman to save all our peoples?"

"All of them?" the other Ajewu said. "And be one people of all our peoples?"

Dabugo waved his hand, and on his signal, Cfradja released her magic and deposited Ioaheaka on the ground. "One people, of this island, for this island."

Ioaheaka looked at him with scorn. "So you will lead us, Withered One?"

"I will fight for you," Dabugo said, taking Ioaheaka's hand and helping him to his feet. "I will save this island, but I have no interest in ruling it."

THE NIGHT HAD COME, AND THE WHITE MOON WAS hidden from view, while the red moon shone high and bright. This was the signal. Dabugo had spent many days and nights going to all the villages of all the peoples who had been pushed toward the beach by the Poasians, and all the peoples who had been pushed upon by them. Agreements were made. Arrangements were planned. He and Cfradja had performed many acts of magic to demonstrate their value to this alliance.

And the word had spread, openly and deliberately. Cfradja had told him the Poasians would play games to learn secrets, which was how her people were defeated. But here, they thought so little of the native people they didn't bother. So the word could be spread to everyone of a time to strike— this night, when the white moon was hidden and the red moon was high and bright.

He moved through the trees, like he was stalking a boar. Cfradja was at his left, where she always was. Further throughout the forest, hunters from the Ajewu, the Gotapa and the Bunaka slipped through the quiet of night.

Just through the tree line was the Poasian

camp. They had formed several of these in the new lands they had claimed. Dabugo wasn't sure why: they built no villages and planted no crops. They just dug holes.

They could see the Poasian soldiers, taking lazy watch around their firepits. Most of them were not wearing their metal shirts— armor, as Cfradja had called it. The snippets of conversation that Dabugo heard were filled with complaints. About the heat, the food, the insects. The kind of thing he had heard from Cfradja in the early days.

Down the tree line, bird calls pierced the air. The signal, the moment. People were in position. That call continued in a line up to the north. It would go for miles, and in each place it was heard, the same thing would happen.

With a wild roar, Dabugo charged out of the trees, as did the hunters to his left and right. They came screaming, spears high, stones slung. They set upon the Poasian soldiers with ferocity. Like sharks in the sea, Dabugo had told them.

That was how he struck. That was how he fought.

Half the Poasians had been asleep. None had been expecting a fight.

The red light of the moon bathed the ground in red. So did Poasian blood.

It was fast, it was brutal.

It was victorious.

"ARE THERE ANY SURVIVORS?" DABUGO ASKED when the fighting ended. "Did any of them surrender, or were subdued?"

"A few," Habedo told him. "I made sure of it, and tied them up."

Survivors were important, at least at this camp, where a message had to be delivered. For the rest of the attacks up the coast, no survivors were needed. None of the people in those battles could speak to the Poasians, anyway. That was left to Dabugo and Cfradja.

"Bring them to me," Dabugo said. "Are we ready?" he asked Cfradja.

She stepped away, her eyes distant. "Yes, I think so. Things are in place. Enough of these battles were won, I believe. The stones are ready."

The stones were Cfradja's idea. She had taken rocks— the right rocks, she insisted, and once Dabugo touched them with his own magic, he could see why— and then carved symbols in them. The stones with the symbols could hold magic, and Dabugo could feel their magic far away. "Beacons," Cfradja had said.

She had made dozens, and they had gone up the coast to all the peoples in this alliance, with the instructions of when to attack. Instructions were given to place the stones in the camps they took.

She placed one of the stones in this camp. Dabugo put his hand on it, and the magic flowed through it into him, and back out to the other stones. He could feel them all, forming a line along the island.

"I'll go to start the charge," Cfradja told him.

"You don't want to tell the messenger?" he asked her. He thought she would relish the chance to spit in the face of a Poasian soldier.

"No," she said. "It's best if they think this is from you. You need them to respect you, Dabugo. If I am part of this, they'll make it about me. And then they'll never give up."

"If you say so."

She kissed his cheek and left his sight.

Habedo brought a Poasian prisoner, whose head was bruised but was otherwise uninjured.

"You fools have no idea what you've done," he said quietly. "You will all be eradicated for this, you befouled skin bags."

"That will not happen," Dabugo told him. The soldier looked surprised.

"So, the monkey skin bag learned a civilized tongue," the soldier said. "I'm not impressed."

"You're going to deliver a message, Poasian," Dabugo said.

"You don't order me. I am a proper man, not a talking beast."

Dabugo ignored him. Cfradja had prepared him for how the Poasians would speak. They would not respect him at all. That didn't matter. What mattered was fear. He squatted down in front of the man, looking him right in the eye, close enough so the man could feel Dabugo's breath on his face.

"In the past, your masters drew a line and told our ancestors that we could not cross that line. And in recent days, you've drawn a new line, taking our lands and places."

"We will take the whole island, beast."

"No," Dabugo said. "Now it is us who will draw a line."

The magic flowed through the stone into Dabugo— Cfradja had started the process. He could feel her, feel the stone, sense all the other stones up the island and down to the river. It was ready.

"And if any of you or yours cross this line," Dabugo said. "You will surely die."

He pushed his magic back into the stone, through the beacons to every stone. He felt Cfradja doing the same, and that magic burst into an orange storm of fire and lightning. It leaped out of the ground, up to the skies, a great wall of magic that every Poasian and native of the island surely saw. In the reddened dark of the night, it shone like an angry sun.

Some of his warriors were on the other side of the line, and despite his assurances of what this was, they still had fear in their eyes. But it didn't matter.

Dabugo reached across the line, the dancing fire of magic and lightning tickling his arm as it passed through. He grabbed the Poasian soldier by the front of his shirt and pulled him into the wall, just for a moment.

The Poasian screamed in agony in that moment, and continued as Dabugo pushed him back down. As the soldier howled, Dabugo signaled to Habedo. Habedo walked through the line as if he were walking from the water to the shore, with painless ease.

Hadebo stomped his feet on the ground, and

raising his spear high he called out a challenge, sneering and spitting on the Poasian.

Then others of the Gotapa, the Ajewu and Kanaka stepped forward, eyes wide and teeth bared. Pounding their chests, they shouted the same refrain.

For anyone of this island, the wall would be a friend.

For the Wuha-No, the Poasians, the invaders, it would be death.

Habedo and the others stepped forward again, shouting the same words.

The Poasian's eyes went wide, gibbering, "What… what are they saying?"

Dabugo smiled. "They say that this is our island, Coconut-man," Dabugo said. "Run and tell your masters that we are taking it back."

CHAPTER 7

DAYS PASSED, AND THE LINE HELD.

The Ajewu and the Bunaka and other tribes moved back to their old spaces, their old villages, and found them much as they left them. The Poasians had disturbed very little, save digging holes.

People were happy.

They wanted to push the line forward, push the Poasians off the island completely. Dabugo wanted that as well, he was certain that was the destiny he was born for. This would be his purpose. But it would take time, patience. He would make his next move when all the peoples on the island were ready.

Dabugo built a hut near the line, slept only a few feet away. The peace was based on this deep magic, magic he had done with Cfradja's teaching, and he felt more comfortable keeping an eye on it.

The Poasians surely were taught the same magic.

Cfradja kept some distance from him for a time, instead traveling north and south down the line. There were times where Dabugo could feel her, making some adjustment to the stones, testing the line. Sometimes he felt she did it just so he would know she was there.

A morning came where he emerged from his hut to find a Poasian waiting on the other side of the line. This man— with his deathly pale skin and hair as black as the darkest night, waited patiently, wearing meticulously clean clothes that must be far too heavy to be comfortable. Dabugo often wondered what sort of place Poasia must be, where people dressed this way. Cfradja had, over the years, tried to describe it, but it was something he simply could not imagine.

"Good morning," the man said. "You are the one responsible for this? And you understand me?"

"Yes to both," Dabugo said in his best Poasian. "Why are you here?"

"To negotiate," the man said. "I must say, we were quite surprised to see magic this sophisticated from the natives here. A barrier that can hurt us, but not you? Quite remarkable."

"So why are you here?" Dabugo asked again.

"As I said, to negotiate. Demolishing this barrier, slaughtering every single one of you, we could do that with minimal effort. Several of my people think we should do just that."

"We will fight you."

"With sticks and stones and a bit of magic," the Poasian said. "The fight would not last for long. Your success was based on surprise. You no longer have that."

Dabugo wasn't sure why, but he felt this man spoke truthfully. What had they told him in his youth? The Dup-No were kind liars, while the Wuha-No were cruel truthtellers.

"So, what do you want?"

"While our retribution would be swift and merciless, minimal effort is not no effort, and it would cost time and lives. We could do that, or we can gain what we require without wasting effort. If you reach agreement with us."

"What sort of agreement?"

The Poasian gave him a little nod. "Good. You're fundamentally willing. I appreciate that there is a spark of civilization in this indecent place. Your people might not be complete wastes of skin."

Dabugo tired of this. "What sort of agreement?"

The man produced a stone, similar to the ones Cfradja had carved her symbols into. "This kind of rock. You are familiar with it? With speckles of purple and red streaks?"

"I've seen many rocks like that."

"Of course, you have," the Poasian said, looking at the carved stone burning within the border line. "It's plentiful in a few groves near here. Places where we were digging."

"You were digging for these stones?"

"Yes, exactly," the man said. "Those stones were the only reason we required the land here. Bring us a few baskets every month, and we won't need to come through here and slaughter all your people."

"Just the stones?" Would they use the stones to break the border? Or did they want them for something else?

"Just the stones," the man said. Then he smiled slightly. "Oh, and the Cthellian woman. Return her to us. She is ours."

. . .

"I WILL NOT GO WITH THEM," CFRADJA SAID. "I would rather die." She had returned from her journey the day after he had spoken with the Poasian. Dabugo wondered if she had stayed away on purpose until this moment. She had told him the Poasians would come and offer a deal. Did she know that they would demand her as part of their payment?

"I don't want to give you to them," Dabugo told her. "I have no intention of doing that. But I had to tell you."

She caressed his face, and looked at the line, the wall of magic and lightning and fire between them and the Poasian side of the island. Now a small contingent of Poasian soldiers waited indifferently on the other side. "I knew this would come. When we did this, they would know I was alive and with you."

"Then why—"

"Because it's the only decent thing I've ever done," she said. She laughed mirthlessly. "My people have been under the Poasian boot for centuries. For so long we've just accepted it. I finally got to fight them back, at least a little."

"Then we'll fight them," Dabugo said.

"You will," she said with a kiss to his cheek.

"We will," he emphasized.

"You will," she said. "As long as I'm here with you, they will not stop. They will shift that wall to kill your people, and push it to the sea. They will tear this island apart to get me. Be certain of that."

"Then together—"

"'Together' was a convenience for us both. For a time," she said. "But that time is done. I cannot be here to help you. And I will not go back to them."

She looked through the wall to the Poasian soldiers. "Do you hear that, *tezhjac?* Tell your masters that I will not go back to you!"

The soldiers took note of her, and one of them looked like he was thinking about a cruel comment to make in response.

She gave a last look to Dabugo, and before he fully understood what she was saying, she said, "I would rather die."

She leaped at the wall.

In a flash, was consumed in the fire and magic.

And Dabugo was alone.

DABUGO CROSSED THE BARRIER WITH HABEDO AT his side, Habedo carrying two baskets full of the special stones. They were special, Dabugo could feel that. Magic flowed through them and pooled around them like nothing else. He couldn't even imagine what they could do with these stones, or what they would do for them.

"Do you think they will honor the deal?" Habedo asked.

"I think they will until they don't. And when that happens, the people of this island need to be ready. We need to be ready."

A small group of Poasian soldiers came with the negotiator. The soldiers silently took the baskets.

"So," the negotiator said. "I'm told the woman is no longer available. This is distressing."

"She killed herself rather than go with you," Dabugo said.

"Unfortunate for your people," the negotiator said. "It's a shame she decided to doom you and yours so selfishly."

"What are they saying?" Habedo asked. He must have been able to tell that this was not going well.

"What will you do, then?" Dabugo asked.

"Without her? Well, we can't fulfill our needs. Someone needs to pay for that."

"We brought you the stones," Dabugo said. "We will bring more."

"Your eagerness to placate me is gratifying," the Poasian man said. "But we needed the stones, as well as a mage of her caliber and talent. Without that—"

"You need a mage?" Dabugo asked. He realized what this meant. Everything that he had endured and learned, it was for this moment right now.

"What is it?" Habedo asked again.

"Quiet," Dabugo told him. "If you had a mage to replace her, does our agreement stand?"

The Poasian raised an eyebrow to that. "Interesting. A bit unconventional for our needs, but interesting." He examined Dabugo like he was a village firetender inspecting a boar carcass. "But, yes, there's power here." He lifted up Dabugo's war blanket and looked at his withered nub of an arm. "And that is… that is an opportunity."

"Does it stand?"

"I think it does," the Poasian said.

"What is happening?" Habedo pleaded.

Dabugo turned to his brother, speaking in their

mother tongue. "Habedo, you need to go back now. You need to go, and keep the people together. All the people of the island. You need to lead them, brother, be the father to all of them. Lead them all in peace, and then be ready when the war comes."

"Me?" Habedo asked. "But why?"

"Because that is your purpose," Dabugo said. "I understand now, brother. We were born together, each for a purpose. The two of us to save our people."

"You make no sense," Habedo said.

"You— strong of arm, tall of body, perfect in form— you were always born to lead. So lead them all."

"And your purpose?"

"As it always has been, brother," Dabugo said. "I was born to be sacrificed, so you could go on to yours. The beach, the day we were born, was not that day. It is today."

Habedo's eyes went wide. He understood. "They're going to take you?"

"They need someone with magic. Cfradja is gone, so it must be me."

"But… who will protect us?"

"You, brother," Dabugo said, touching his brother's face for the last time. He was surprised that there were tears streaming from his brother's eyes. And from his own. "This agreement will hold, until it doesn't. When they decide to break it, when my life stops buying you time, you have to be ready."

"How long will that be?" Habedo asked. "Are they going to kill you?"

"I don't think they will. But my life now will belong to them, until they're done with it. Perhaps that was always my purpose, to be used by them. But with that purpose, I'm buying you time, brother. Use it well."

Habedo took Dabugo by the hand— his withered hand— and squeezed it with affection. Nothing more could be said. Then he went back into the jungle.

Dabugo had been abandoned on the beach on the day he was born. He did not die that day, as he was needed by the world to serve a great purpose. And now on this day, for all his people, that purpose would be served.

ACKNOWLEDGMENTS

So here we are with a very new adventure, on several levels. We have new characters in the center, we're outside of Maradaine, and we're publishing in a new way. All of this has been a journey, and I'm thrilled to share it with you.

That journey was shepherded by the work I've been doing on my podcast Worldbuilding for Masochists, and I can't express how much my co-hosts, Rowenna Miller and Cass Morris, are just the best people to work with. Brilliant, creative minds, and incredible anchors of support. More support came from patrons and fans, like Brian Yost and Ember Randall.

Absolutely essential for this book was Britta Jensen, who helped midwife every aspect of this book. Very grateful for her counsel, advise, expertise and friendship.

Also instrumental were my usual sounding boards: Daniel Fawcett, forever my absolute rock when it comes to every element of this saga; and

Miriam Robinson Gould, the best first reader I could ask for.

On top of that, my family remains a source of strength and inspiration. This includes my parents Nancy and Lou, and my mother-in-law Kateri. And, of course, my son Nicholas and wife Deidre, who have continued to put up with me during this incredible journey through Maradaine and beyond.

And thank you, dear reader. Because you have this book in your hands, you've joined me on this newest journey, and I'm so thrilled to have you with me.

About the Author

Marshall Ryan Maresca is a fantasy and science-fiction writer, author of the Maradaine Saga: Four braided series set amid the bustling streets and crime-ridden districts of the exotic city called Maradaine, which includes The *Thorn of Dentonhill, A Murder of Mages, The Holver Alley Crew* and *The Way of the Shield*, as well as the dieselpunk fantasy, *The Velocity of Revolution*. He is also the co-host of the Hugo-nominated, Stabby-winning podcast **Worldbuilding for Masochists**, and has been a playwright, an actor, a delivery driver and an amateur chef. He lives in Austin, Texas with his family.

9 781958 743065